Christmas Kringle

Tales from Biders Clump Book 1

Danni Roan

Copyright © 2016 Danni Roan

ISBN-10: 1520710054
ISBN-13: 978-1520710051

Cover design by: JessicaArt

Library of Congress Control Number: 2018675309
Printed in the United States of America

Contents

Prologue

"Sara, be careful," Maud Adams called, twitching the long rope in her hands.

"Mama, I'm fine," a cheerful voice shot back from the darkness beneath the limbs of the tall evergreen.

"Mama, let go of the rope, you'll pull her down."

Sara could hear her sister's voice echo up toward her. "Prissy, don't distract her," Maude chided.

"Mama," Aquila's voice was quiet and Sara could feel the rope tied to her waist shiver as her oldest sister took it from her mother's hands. Mama always fussed too much.

"Sara has climbed trees before, she will be fine." Leave it to Quil to be rational.

"I know, but this time she's so far up."

Wrapping one leg around the tree's base, Sara pulled the small handsaw from her belt and began drawing its sharp teeth back and forth along the rough bark of the fragrant evergreen. She loved the smell of pine, the feel of the tiny threads of sawdust as they sifted onto her hand.

Snow that had settled onto the upper limbs of the tree shivered with every draw of the blade and sifted down onto her head, making her giggle.

Sara Adams, the youngest daughter of Maude Adams, loved to climb trees and despite the unlady-like reputation it fostered, she continued to do it even at the age of seventeen. In recent years she had learned to keep this favorite pastime a secret, but she still indulged as often as she could in the deep woods behind her home.

"I'm almost through," she called, looking down the tall trunk at her family below. Her mother, sil-very hair piled loosely on her head, turned wor-ried eyes upward, wringing her hands with concern while Priscilla and Aquila's bright eyes shown with merriment.

"Let me tie it off and when I'm done, you give it a good tug." Sara smiled, her eyes twinkling at the fun of cutting this particular tree top. It would be the perfect Christmas tree, its sloping branches thick with dark green needle and speckled with tiny cones.

"There!" she called, securing the knot and trying to shimmy away.

She felt the rope spring tight a second too soon, her grip on the thin trunk slipping as the trunk cracked like a rifle shot, tipped, and bounced off her shoulder.

Sara felt herself falling and pushed away from the rough limbs and toppling treetop, sending her body into the open air. Her mother's panicked scream was the last thing she heard as the icy wind whistled past her ears.

Chapter 1

"Seraphina! Seraphina!" The frantic calls in her mother's voice broke through the ringing in her ears as Sara gasped for breath, opening her eyes.

"Easy there now," a warm baritone voice vibrated through her as her stomach clenched trying to aid her lungs in drawing air. "You got the wind knocked out of ya," the man leaning over her continued, his warm hand coming to rest on her abdomen.

Sara felt like she was dying, felt like all of the air in the world had been drawn away into space and this angel had come to take her home.

A warm, sharp pressure on her middle caused a groan to jump from her throat, then blessed cold, biting air filled her lungs.

"There ya go." The man's voice tickled her ears. "Just breathe." She felt his arm slip beneath her knees, causing the rough fabric of her father's trousers to bunch around her ankles as she gazed into soft brown eyes.

Gently he lifted her legs, then laid them straight

again, causing her lungs to draw more air even as her long, calico skirt pooled around her hips.

Sara's heart seemed to beat a little faster as a smile broke out across the stranger's handsome face. "Do you think you can stand?" he whispered, his brown eyes never leaving hers. She nodded.

With gentle hands, he helped her to her feet, a strong arm supporting her as her head spun. "Are you hurt?"

"Seraphina Adams!" Her mother's sharp words cut through the spell that the man's eyes had cast. "How could you have worried me so?" Tears sparkled in her mother's eyes and Sara turned to look at her.

"I'm alright, Mama," she answered, her voice sounding raspy.

"Mrs. Adams," the man said, drawing all eyes back to him. "She only had the wind knocked out of her. This fresh snow saved her from any real harm." He stretched his hand wide to encompass the vast area of white.

Sara watched as the young man tipped his gray Stetson back on his head of sandy hair and looked up at the decapitated pine. "That's a far ways to fall, though," he added, shaking his head. "You're one lucky young woman."

Sara smiled, thinking that she truly was lucky, especially with this handsome man's arm still wrapped securely around her waist.

"If you don't mind my asking, what were you doing cutting the top out of that particular tree anyway?"

"That's none of your business, Rafe Dixon," Maude barked, taking Sara by the arm and dragging her away from the man's warmth and strength. "It's my tree and we'll do whatever we want with it."

Rafe Dixon pushed his hat back again until it barely rested on the back of his head and scratched at his temple. He'd been out riding fence when he'd heard the older woman scream and flogged his pony to the rescue. As his cow horse had made the last leap over the drifted snow, he'd watched in awe as the pretty girl with the long, red curls had plopped with a humph into the snow.

He'd not given a thought to where he was or who he was with, but had leapt from the saddle, kneeling next to the prostrate figure as she'd gasped for breath.

"Ma'am," his voice was hesitant. "I'm not so sure that is your tree," he said, ducking his head at the sharp look the older woman gave him.

"I think I know my own tree," Mrs. Adam's spat, her blue eyes flashing as she placed hands on hips and leaned toward him.

"I'm just saying that it's mighty close to our land,"

he tried, his voice reasonable.

Maude Adams raised an index finger, preparing to give the young man a piece of her mind.

"It doesn't matter now," Quil spoke, placing a soothing hand on her mother's arm. "All that matters is that Sara's all right." Her voice was beyond reasonable as she pulled her mother away.

Sara rested a hand on Mr. Dixon's arm. "Thank you for your help," she said sweetly, her green eyes doing something funny to his head.

"What kind of knight in shining armor would I be if I didn't come to the rescue of the damsel in distress?" he smiled mischievously.

"Are you sure the damsel needed rescuing?" Sara asked, her smile matching his. Behind them, her sisters were wrapping the tree with the rope they'd used to pull it down. "I think Aquila may have rescued you just now." She nodded at her mother.

Rafe shook his head. "Your ma sure got riled up about the tree, didn't she?" he asked, placing his hand over hers where it rested on the sleeve of his heavy winter coat.

"I'm afraid our families have never been very friendly," Sara agreed.

Rafe nearly choked on his laugh. "That's an understatement." He looked down at her small hand.

"Your hands are cold," he said, rubbing it gently.

Sara looked into his dark eyes and sighed.

"Seraphina Adams, you come along now." Her mother's words were terse, grumpy.

"Yes, Ma'am," the girl replied, slowly pulling her hand away. "Thank you again," she said and trudged through the snow to grasp the rope with her sisters, dragging the pine over the soft white glitter of the snow.

As the voices of the women faded behind him, Rafe looked up, up, up to where the tall tree had been neatly topped. "Fools and children," he muttered, judging the point of separation to be at least thirty feet in the air.

Only Seraphina Adams was definitely no child. He replayed the scene in his head again, wishing to preserve it clearly for future review. The lean young woman had fallen from the tree without a sound.

He wondered if he would have known anything was amiss if Mrs. Adams hadn't screamed.

Riding into that tiny clearing, his breath had been taken away as he watched the slim, red-haired angel fall to earth. Her arms had been spread wide, her faded skirts fluttering in the wind caused by her descent, and she'd landed with only the slightest grunt, leaving a perfect impression in the snow.

Walking to his horse, Rafe pulled the reins into his hands and swung aboard, turning to study the spot where only moments ago he'd knelt over the prostrate young woman. He chuckled to himself, understanding now why she'd worn britches under her skirts.

How anyone could climb a tree like that was beyond him. Squinting his eyes against the glare of the sun reflected on the winter-white forest, he could just make out the huddled figures of the four women as they headed to their home on the other side of the rise.

He smiled again as his eyes followed the strange trail the treetop and their heavy skirts had left in the snow.

A soft wind stirred, blowing flicks of snow into his face and Rafe shivered, buttoning the front of his heavy sheepskin and leather coat. With a sigh, he reached in his pocket for his gloves and pulled out not a pair, but one poor lonely mitt.

Shaking his head, he patted his speckled pony's neck. "Looks like I lost another one, Chester," he said with a groan as he turned his horse toward home, a pair of sparkling green eyes dancing in his head.

Chapter 2

Sara wiped the last dish dry and settled it onto the shelf with the others, then turned to gaze out the window at the row of white birch trees that bordered their yard. The tall trees' bare branches swayed in a soft breeze and a flicker of white caught her eye.

Looking around the quiet kitchen to see that no one was there, she lifted her heavy coat from its peg by the back door and silently slipped out into the frosty snow.

Through the trunks of the trees, she caught a glimpse of brown and the flick of a horse's whitetail.

"Mr. Dixon," she called, stuffing her hands in her pockets as she stepped through the trees. A tall Appaloosa bobbed its head at her, huffing softly and causing steam to trail from its nostrils into the crisp air.

"Ms. Adams?" Rafe stepped around his horse, a small, bent pick in his hand that he'd been using to pull clods of snow from his horse's hooves. "I was wondering how you were doing?" he offered shyly. "After your fall, I mean."

"Oh, I'm fine," Sara smiled, "I've had worse falling out of bed." She blushed, realizing what she'd said, but the handsome young cowboy only smiled.

"Why didn't you come up to the house?" Sara continued, studying his face as she stroked his horse's neck.

"I didn't know if your Ma would let me in," Rafe replied honestly, "and after the night I had with my Pa…" He shook his head disgustedly.

"What happened?" Sara's eyes were wide with worry. "Surely he wasn't angry with you for helping us?"

"He had a downright conniption when I told him what happened." He ducked his head at the memory. "He said he's gonna go to the sheriff about your Ma cuttin' down his tree."

Sara gasped. Would old Mr. Dixon do that? "But I thought that was our tree," she said lamely.

Rafe shrugged, twisting his hat in his hand. "I don't see what the big deal is, either way," he offered. "I mean, it's just a tree, and taking a bit off the top won't hurt." He lifted his brown eyes to hers and Sara's heart skipped a beat.

"Do you even know why my Ma and your father

are at such odds with each other?" she asked, hoping that for once in her life she'd get a straight answer to this question.

"I have no idea," Rafe said, his voice echoing the same confusion she felt. "All I know is something happened a long time ago and neither one of them has been able to stand each other since."

"It seems silly to hold a grudge for so long," Sara said, shoving her hand into the pocket of her winter coat.

"Are you cold?" Rafe asked, stepping close, his breath making soft wisps of steam in the air as he rested his hands on her arms.

"I'm alright," Sara replied. It was nice standing here in the snow, talking to him. "If it's any consolation, the treetop makes a beautiful Christmas tree," she offered with a smile.

"So that's what you wanted it for."

"Why else would I go to all that trouble?" Sara laughed. She looked down at his hands where they rested on her arms. "Where are your gloves?" she asked, turning her eyes toward his.

"I must have lost one," he said, stepping back to clear his head. For a minute, he'd been tempted to kiss the girl. He'd only come to see that she was alright. He reached into his pocket and pulled out the one forlorn glove and dangled it before her.

"Oh dear, that's terrible. Did you lose it when you were helping me?"

"Maybe, I don't know. I had it when I was riding fence, but you get on and off so many times there's no telling when I dropped it." He patted his horse on the rump. "Poor Chester here could probably ride the fence line himself, we've done it so many times."

"Why'd your father build that fence, anyway?" Sara asked, her bright eyes inquisitive.

Rafe's face heated, "He said he didn't want any of your raggedy…" He paused, realizing what his father had said, exactly. "Your, ah, ragged cattle mixing with his."

Sara scowled, her soft brows the same deep reddish-brown of her hair drawing downward. "Our cattle aren't raggedy," she mused. "They're all good stock and well-cared for."

"According to my father, nothing good can ever come off this patch of land." His brown eyes were warm as they studied Sara's face, and he couldn't help but think that something very good had come from this little bit of earth.

"Do you feel the same way?" Sara asked. "Do you think we're worthless?" Her voice was a troubled whisper.

"No," he answered simply, running a finger along the edge of her cheek. "I think some mighty fine stock can be found in these parts."

Sara dipped her head, feeling suddenly shy, a feeling that was altogether unfamiliar.

Rafe took a step back from the pretty young woman he was so drawn to. *How had he never noticed her before?* He'd been away a couple of years to study, but the rest of his life he'd lived right next door to the Adams clan, and Sara had somehow completely eluded his notice.

"I'd better get moving," he commented, his voice soft. "I'm glad you're alright," he added, smiling.

"Thank you for coming by," Sara offered awkwardly. "Perhaps I'll see you around town." Her green eyes were hopeful.

"That'd be nice," Rafe replied, running the dark leather reins through his fingers and wishing it was her hair instead.

Chester, growing impatient, tossed his head and snorted, tugging on the reins, making both Rafe and Sara smile.

"Good night, then," Sara finally spoke as he swung into the saddle and turned away.

For several moments Sara watched the tall, lean cowboy on the white horse with the black and brown spots as they melded into the gathering dusk of a winter's night. She shivered delightedly as she headed back to the warmth of the house.

Chapter 3

"You each have your money?" Maud Adams questioned, looking up at her daughters as she pulled her gloves a little snugger on her hands.

They were all bundled up for their trip to town and her fingers tingled from the cold. Driving the buggy always left her fingers cold in weather like this.

"Yes, Mama," all three girls replied, gazing around the sleepy streets of Biders Clump.

"Good, now don't be wasteful, but I hope you'll all have something special to share for Christmas. Things are still a little tight until next round up," she added, smoothing the vast expanse of gray fabric that made up her skirt. The dress itself was at least five years out of style but was still pretty.

"I'm headed to the post office first to send letters, but we'll meet for lunch at the Grist Mill at noon." She tilted her head, exposing her cheek and each young woman placed a kiss as expected before scurrying off to do their own shopping.

"Mind you stay out of trouble," Maud shot as an after-thought as Sara gave her a perfunctory kiss and stepped off the boardwalk.

Sara sighed as she left her mother behind. On the far side of the street, she could see Aquila striding toward the tiny book shop. Quil was four years older than Sara, and book smart as well as pretty. She had dark brown hair streaked with gold and dark green eyes that grew darker depending on her mood.

Sara always felt like the runt next to Quil, who towered over her at five feet eight inches. She'd once heard a dressmaker refer to Aquila as regal.

Further along, she could make out Pricilla as she stepped into the mercantile, her blonde bun bouncing with her jaunty step. Prissy, Sara's senior by only two years, was shorter even than Sara, standing only five foot four in her stocking feet. Prissy's smaller stature seemed to run to plump but with all the soft curves Sara's lacked.

Sara was the tomboy of the family. She'd always preferred being outdoors with the animals to household chores, and when her father had been alive, she'd often ridden with him until the sun made her nose freckle, and her hair shine with golden light. She sighed, missing her father.

Even though Mr. Adams had been gone for nearly five years, his absence was keenly felt, and never more than at the holidays.

Not wanting to follow Pricilla into the store when she was doing her Christmas shopping, Sara turned down the street, looking in windows as she moved through town.

"Mornin'," a soft, husky voice called as Sara approached the boarding house.

"Good morning, Miss Polly Esther," Sara said with a smile.

"In ta do the Chris'mas shoppin' I see," the older woman spoke from her rocking chair on the porch of the boarding house.

"Yes," Sara replied, while the woman's keen blue eyes assessed her.

"I was sorry to hear of your troubles this fall," Polly Esther, one of the town's oldest matrons, said. her voice holding no pity or censure.

"Thank you," Sara replied, unsure what to say. Miss Polly was a fixture in Biders Clump and if she wasn't bustling about in her kitchen, working at the church, or tending to her guests, she could usually be found sitting in her old, bentwood rocker by her door.

"Where's Mr. George today?" Sara asked, trying to avoid her family's most recent embarrassment.

"Outback choppin' wood." The old woman smiled, tucking a strand of hair behind her ears as her sharp, blue eyes softened. "He keeps busy most days," she added with a slight smile.

"I'm surprised to see you out here on such a cold morning," Sara said, grinning at Polly. She wondered what it would be like to be married to the same man for forty years and still twinkle at the mere thought of him.

A vision of a lean, sandy-haired cowboy on a spotted horse came to mind, and her cheeks flushed.

"There goes that Bruno," Polly Esther's words caught Sara by surprise, and she turned to see the dark-haired young man trailing along behind Janine Williams.

"That boy follows her around like a lost pup and she ain't got the sense to see him for what he is."

"What is he?" Sara asked, suddenly curious.

Polly's whole face lit up and she offered a sideways wink. "Mostly a silly boy in love with a silly girl," she answered, "but mark my words, that boy will be something someday. He's got notions."

"Like what?" Sara was truly curious now.

"Oh, never you mind about that. For now, you just keep your eyes peeled to see what happens. That Janine Williams is full of herself, what with her pa being the banker and all, but the chit hasn't got the sense God gave a goose, and I mean no disrespect to the goose." She wobbled her head, making her white-gold hair bobble.

"Who you jawin' with?" A man's deep voice came around the side of the two-story building followed by George, his arms full of wood.

"Good morning, Mr. George," Sara said, offering the man a bright smile.

"Mornin' Sara," The older man grinned. His dark hair, streaked with white, was damp from his morning work. "You in ta do yer Christmas shoppin?"

"Yes, sir."

"I was tellin' young Sara here ta keep an eye on Bruno," Polly said, nodding toward where the man in cowboy boots and a ragged coat trailed behind the girl with the chestnut hair.

"That girl ain't got no sense at all," George echoed what Polly had said only moments ago.

"You mark my words now, George," Polly said with a grin, "he'll marry her anyway."

"If you say so," George agreed, offering a wink with a hooded brown eye. "I don't suppose you could help me with a few mornin' chores could ya?" the boarding house proprietor asked. "These cold mornings is kinda hard on my lumbago," he added, looking at Sara.

"Oh, yes," Sara agreed, "I'd be glad to help. What

can I do?"

George smiled brightly. "Let's start with cleaning up the woodpile a bit," he said, stacking what he had in his arms at the door and turning down the alley toward the back yard.

Sara was surprised at the piles and piles of wood George had stacked along the small barn at the back of the property. A large chopping stump stood nearby with an ax stuck in it and she suddenly hoped she wouldn't need to chop the large pieces she saw before her.

"Here, ya better put this on," the old man offered, handing her a heavy apron. "Now if you'll fetch that pail and start pickin' up the splits and kindling,' I'd be much obliged. I don't like all that bendin' and stooping," he added, placing a foot on the stump and pulling the ax free with one hand.

"Of course," Sara agreed, then set about collecting the twigs, bark, and branches that had flown about the yard.

The steady thwack, thwack of the ax falling filled the small space as she worked. Mr. George seemed quite strong for his age.

"That looks pretty good," he called several minutes later as her bucket began to fill. "You carry that on into the kitchen and put it in the tinder box." He hefted several split logs and turned toward the door at the back of the house.

Inside, George began stacking the wood in a small alcove near a large cook stove. "Just put it right in there," he said. The small wooden box stood to the other side of the stove and carefully Sara began arranging the slivers of wood so they'd be within easy reach.

Finally emptying her bucket, she turned toward the door to see a heavy coat hanging on a peg. It was bright blue with big buttons on the sleeves and dangling from each sleeve, by a pretty ribbon, was a bright red mitten.

"You like Polly's extra coat?" George asked with a chuckle.

"I was noticing the mittens," Sara replied honestly.

"My Polly Esther is a wonderful woman," George began. "She's a fantastic cook, a loving wife, and a superb mother," he said, "but she can't keep track of her gloves to save her life. I've worried too many years about frostbite, so's a few years ago I sewed them mittens up with ribbon and stitched 'em to her sleeves." He chuckled. "Now she's snug as a bug in a rug when she goes out on really cold days."

Sara smiled. It was sweet to see the older man taking such care of his wife.

"Now what'a I owe ya for yer help today?" he asked.

"That's alright," Sara said flushing. "I'm glad to help."

"Nonsense," the old man scoffed, "a workman is worthy of his hire." He pulled a shiny silver coin from his pocket and tossed it to her. She gasped as she snatched it from the air, surprised she had caught it.

"Now you run along and finish up that Christmas shopping," George said with a wink and shooed her out the door.

Chapter 4

The little bell over the door of the mercantile tinkled - there always seemed to be a little bell - as Sara stepped into the warm, aromatic depth of the local store.

"Mornin' Miss Sara," Mr. Bentley called as he dusted off a shelf at the back of the room. "Prissy was in a minute ago, are you looking for her?" he asked solicitously.

"No, I'm in to do some shopping of my own," she replied, running her hand along

the table with the brightly colored fabrics on their long skeins.

"Ah, Christmas," he said knowingly, laying a finger along his nose. "I've got some lovely new parcels, arrived this morning."

"I think I'll look around a bit," Sara offered, turning and walking toward the tall shelves where on a previous occasion she'd seen a writing set her oldest sister had admired. The small, pink box near the top of the shelf was wrapped with a satin ribbon and contained paper, pen, and ink.

The bell on the door tinkled again as she stretched up to get a finger under the box. She hated to make Mr. Bentley leave his other customer. A large hand shifted over her head, grasped the box, then lowered it to her.

"Thank you," she said brightly, turning to see who'd been kind enough to help. Her smile widened as she looked up into the handsome face of Rafe Dixon.

"Ma'am," he drawled, tipping his hat with two fingers.

"I came in to pick up Pa's order," he offered in way of explanation to his presence but didn't step back from where he stood gazing down at her.

Sara dropped her eyes and studied the small box in her hand.

"It's mighty pretty," Rafe offered, his eyes still on her face.

"I was thinking of getting it for my sister," Sara said. "She likes to write and helps keep the books for the ranch." She smiled shyly, realizing he probably didn't care about the box or the books.

"You here for that order your Pa placed, Rafe?" Mr. Bentley called from where he was busy laying out items on the long counter.

"Yes, sir," Rafe replied politely, turning to address the shop keeper. "Is it ready?" He couldn't help but feel disgruntled at the interruption.

"I'll have it for you in a jiffy." Mr. Bentley pushed his glasses up his aquiline nose and reached for several items on the shelf behind him.

"No rush," Rafe said with a grin.

"Mr. Bentley," Sara called softly, once again studying the pretty box. "How much is this writing set?"

"That'd be two-dollars, Ms. Sara," the clerk replied, glancing over his shoulder before returning to his work.

Rafe watched as the young woman flushed prettily, then turned to put the box back on the shelf. "I'm not sure Quil would like pink," she said absently.

Rafe took the box from her hands and lifted it back up to the spot on the shelf from where he'd removed it only moments ago.

"What kind of things does your sister like?" he asked, following as Sara began perusing the shelves once more.

"Books mostly," Sara said softly. "We all enjoy reading, but Quil will buy each of us a book this year," she added. "She buys us a book every year," she finished with a grin.

Her hand traced the soft, brightly colored calicos and chintzes as she passed the fabrics table again. She wished she could afford a few yards for her mother, but this year money was entirely too tight.

Rafe studied Ms. Adams with interest, suddenly noticing the frayed hem of her skirt and the rough edge on the toe of her sensible boots as they peeked out from under her faded dress. Her coat, though well-cleaned, also showed signs of wear.

"My Ma always liked trinkets," he mused, taking the girl's elbow and ushering her to another shelf. "One time when I was small, I found this box of stamps and bought her one."

From the very bottom shelf at the far end of the room, he pulled out a square, wooden box with small carved objects scattered haphazardly inside. He reached in and pulled one out. It looked tiny between his thick square fingers. "See."

Turning the object, he showed the flat bottom where a simple image had been etched into a rubber pad. "You roll them in ink and then you can make a mark on any paper."

Sara smiled, seeing how the little objects worked. "What kind of pictures do they have?" she asked, her eyes shining with excitement as she began digging through the box.

"All sorts of things," he said, lifting them one at a time and examining the simple pictures. "Pa thought they were silly, but Ma loved them." His smile widened as he turned the handle over on one stamp, showing her the image.

"It's a quill," she squealed, taking it from his hands and holding it to the light. A long shaggy feather had been carved into the brown rubber which had been glued to the short wooden shaft. "It's perfect," she gushed.

Rafe had never wanted to kiss someone so badly in his life. His whole heart seemed to be trying to crawl out of his chest in delight at Sara's enthusiasm.

"Mr. Bentley?" Sara called, dashing to the front of the store. "How much for this stamp?"

"Those silly old things?" the man blinked, adjusting his glasses to look at them. "Twenty-cents apiece," he said. "I'm lettin' em go at cost. Silliest things the missus ever picked up, if you ask me."

"I'll have this one," Sara enthused. "It's perfect."

"Your order's ready," Mr. Bentley directed at Rafe as he shook his head at the girl's choice. "This all you're gettin'?" he asked Sara, who flushed anew.

"Oh my, no," she said, giggling at her distraction. "I still need to find something for Ma and Pricilla."

"Prissy was sure eyeing that set of ribbons over there," Mr. Bentley offered, pointing toward another table.

Sara turned to look at the ribbons, bumping into Rafe where he'd walked up behind her. She giggled, not feeling the slightest bit embarrassed at the contact. "I'm sorry," she said politely, though.

"I'm not." Rafe's words barely reached her ears and she gasped at his forwardness.

"Here ya go, Mr. Dixon," the shopkeeper said, wresting two heavy sacks onto the table.

"Thank you," Rafe said, unenthusiastically stepping away from Sara and hefting the bags before turning for the door. "Merry Christmas," he added, setting the bell to chime as he exited.

After Rafe left the store, Sara picked out a few ribbons for Pricilla and a pair of soft gloves for her mother, but with her final silver dollar, she purchased several strings of finished leather, tucking them into her pocket silently as she left to meet her family.

Rafe stood in the stable door, watching as Sara Adams hustled across the chilly street toward the Grist Mill Café. She held three small packaged wrapped in brown paper and string and he wondered what her Christmas would be like.

His eyes followed her as she stepped onto the porch of the small restaurant. He had the sudden urge for a cup of coffee, but instead strapped his supplies to his horse's saddle, thinking.

"Ain't no Santa Clause left no more," Byron Breaks' voice filtered into the barn from his small office at the front of the hostelry.

"That's just ain't so," another voice argued. "I seen him myself."

Rafe chuckled. Leave it to George to say such a thing.

"Ain't nobody ever seen Santa Claus," Byron grumbled. "He's on'y one of them fairy tales folks tell their kids."

"I can't argue with that," George said reasonably, "but that ain't what I mean. It's your turn, by the way."

"Don't rush me." Byron's voice was gruff as he studied the checkerboard Rafe was sure sat before them. "An' what'a ya mean that ain't what ya mean."

"We tell our youngin's about Santa and his presents, but it's more than that," George answered patiently. "It's about givin', or it should be anyway."

"People are plain silly," Byron grouched again.

"People are people," George said. "Tellin' children there is a Santa is a little bit of fiction that teaches them about giving and that this world can be beautiful, wonderful, and magical if we look."

"Fiction hey? Kina' like some of them tall tales Polly Esther likes ta tell," Byron chortled, but there was no heat in his words.

"I reckon that's Polly's way of bringin' a little cheer into our world. You ever seen her tellin' the kids stories?" he asked, his voice full of pride. "Why them little ones at Sund'y School is practically spell-bound and them stories teach youngin's how to behave and do what's right."

"She sure can spin a yarn," Byron admitted.

"I reckon Santa's like that, too." George must have leaned back in his chair because it squeaked and protested under his bulk. "It gives us someone else ta blame for our good deeds. We can go 'round spreading Christmas cheer with impunity."

"What's that mean?" Byron barked. "It don't sound healthy."

"It's when folks don't know you done something, but you do," George said. "Now you gonna play or not?"

Rafe draped the reins of his spotted horse around a post, patted the animal on the neck, and strode away down the street. The bell above the mercantile door jangled loudly as he entered for the second time, never seeing the two whiteheads that peeped out of the stable office door grinning widely.

Chapter 5

"Maud Adams," Harlan Dixon drawled, his voice high and nasally as if he'd smelled something unpleasant. "What brings you to town?" he asked, pulling a silver watch from his brocade vest pocket.

"Mr. Dixon," the older woman said tersely, "it's nice to see you well." If her tone of voice was any indication, her feelings on the matter were a completely opposite to her words.

"Dinning out, Maud?" The man looked down his nose. "I'm surprised that with your little problem recently that you can afford it."

Maud Adams lifted her napkin from her place setting and spread it carefully across her lap. "We manage, Harlan," she said stiffly. "Do have a good day." Her words were an obvious dismissal, but the man ignored them.

"Why don't you sell me that ramshackle place you call a ranch?" he snapped. "I'll even pay top dollar for the crow-bait creatures you call cows." His dark eyes gleamed menacingly.

Sara walked into the small dining room of the Grist Mill to see her mother talking to Harlan Dixon. She could see by the red flush on her mother's face that the conversation was not going well. It seemed that almost every time the two of them crossed paths, sparks flew.

"My home is not for sale, Mr. Dixon," Maud barked, her dark blue eyes flashing with anger. "I don't know how many times I have to tell you that. You would think a man of your breeding and education would be able to grasp such a simple concept." Her icy expression chilled the room.

Mr. Dixon bridled, jerking his long, black coat straight with an irritated tug. "You always were a stubborn woman, Maude," he snapped, then turned on his heel and stepped through the door, never even acknowledging Sara's presence.

"Mama?" Sara hurried to her mother and slipped into a chair next to her. She could see the tears building in the deep blue depths of the eyes that had only ever shown her love.

"It's alright," Maude said, dabbing at her eyes. "That man is still the most odious creature I've ever met." She forced a smile for her youngest child. "Did you finish your shopping?"

"Yes," Sara said, thinking about her encounter with Rafe and deciding that there were some things that her mother didn't need to know. "Did you post your letters?"

"I did, it was so busy in the office. People sending last-minute packages, Christmas cards, and letters." She smiled brightly, the distress from a moment ago fading. "It was very festive."

The main door opened again as Prissy stepped inside, spotted them, and joined the tiny group already at the table. "What a lovely day for shopping," Prissy said, smiling. "Did you find anything nice?" she asked, her soft gray eyes cheerful. "I saw the cutest things. I believe we have one of the best mercantile anywhere."

Prissy always seemed to be able to find the bright side of things and her cheerful nature was often down-right contagious.

"Christmas is right around the corner," Maud said. "It's always such a special time of year." She took her daughter's hand, patting it gently, but Sara noted the worry lines around her eyes.

"I do hope Quil comes along soon," Pricilla said, looking around the nearly empty café. "She can get lost in a book, that one," she added, but her smile was sweet.

"Why don't we order some tea while we wait?" Maud offered, raising her hand to catch a server's eye.

"Should we, Mama?" Sara whispered.

"It will be like old times when we used to come to town for tea each week and meet with friends."

Sara smiled, remembering. It had been like a fancy party to her when she was small, and even though she had to put on her best dress, she always enjoyed it. There had been no tea parties since her father had passed away five years ago.

A cool breath of air drifted across the room as Aquila entered, carrying a heavy bag in one hand. Prissy winked at Sara, who giggled. They all knew that Quil would buy books. She always did, after all.

"Oh, tea," Aquila said., her voice rich and smoky.

"Yes, we'll call it a Christmas treat," Mrs. Adams said. "It's been far too long."

The tea and luncheon truly were festive as the four women chatted and discussed plans for the week. They would all be helping with the Christmas play and other community events and had much to do.

As their simple meal was served, Sara looked out the window and saw Rafe Dixon leaving the general store. She wondered if he'd forgotten something earlier and had to return. She also wondered when she might see the handsome cowboy next.

With the tensions between their two families, she and Rafe had lived their whole lives in the same town but had barely ever seen each other. That was a real shame, to her way of thinking.

"Sara?" her mother's voice brought her back from her musings and she blinked, wondering what she'd missed. "Is your meal alright?" her mother asked, looking at her with concern.

"Oh, yes," she said, lifting a forkful of chicken to her lips. "It's lovely."

***

It was Sara's week to wash dishes, so for the second day in a row, she found herself staring out the window toward the trees. A bright red cardinal fluttered in, landing on a branch of one of the birch trees, its crimson feathers a riot of color in a white world.

Sara watched the bird but also watched for a flash of a whitetail or the tawny brown of a heavy coat, but she saw nothing. It was unrealistic for her to have hoped that Rafe might have found some time to call on her, but she'd still hoped.

Carefully she dried the dishes and put them away, replaying their earlier conversation in the store. He certainly was a handsome young man.

"Sara, what are you doing in there?" her mother's voice carried from the small parlor on the other side of the door.

"I'm finishing up now," she replied, turning away

from the window as the little red bird fluttered away.

"Sara, why don't you make us some fudge?" Priscila's voice bubbled from where she sat by a small fire, knitting.

"That would be lovely," Maud said, smiling at her youngest. "We have everything we need for it."

"Alright," Sara giggled at their pleading. She'd found the recipe for the new confection in the newspaper several months before, and it had instantly become a favorite with her family.

Still, in good spirits, she turned back to the wood-burning stove and added fuel, then pulled down a heavy saucepan and measured out a cup of butter from the icebox. It wasn't long until she had butter, milk, and sugar boiling in the pan and added cocoa powder and heavy cream.

Her arms ached while she stirred as the thick, sweet concoction began to set and she quickly poured it into a buttered tin. She loved making fudge. It was her specialty.

"I'm going to put this out on the sill to cool," she called to her mother, grabbing a heavy shawl and stepping out the door onto the porch. The pan was warm in her hands and she held it close, enjoying the contrasting cold and heat.

The sun was a thin line along the horizon as

night's icy fingers inched across the forest, turning the snow to blue and gold.

"Sara," the gruff whisper drifted toward her on the crisp air.

"Rafe, is that you?" she answered, careful not to be heard by anyone in the cabin.　　She stepped into the snow, still holding the pan, looking for him. "Where are you?"

"Here," he called, his voice full of teasing.

Sara walked further into the yard. To her right on the other side of the cabin, she could see the barn.

An icy hand grabbed her arm, and she bit down hard to stop a yelp of fright as he pulled her behind a stubby pine.

"What are you doing here?" Sara whispered, glancing back at the little cabin.

"There's no livin' with Pa tonight," Rafe said with a scowl. "He's raging around the house like a blue northern."

Sara dropped her eyes. "Is it because he saw Mother in town today?" she asked, her voice sad.

"I'm afraid so," he offered softly, then placed his finger under her chin and lifted her eyes to his. "It's not your fault, you know. This feud has been going on for a long time."

"I know, but it is so unlike my mother to hold things against people."

"My Pa's not all bad, either," he said, lightening his words with a smile. "He's a tough businessman and a fierce worker, but he's fair, even generous sometimes.

Sara's eyes were wide with disbelief and Rafe used his finger to lift her chin, closing her mouth that now hung open.

"I know, it's hard to believe," he said. "When he gets like this, he's impossible."

"Do you have any idea why they despise each other so?" Sara asked. "I can't understand."

Rafe shook his head. "I have no idea and if you ask Pa, he goes off on a tangent about untrustworthy folks and double-crossing people."

"You don't think that of my mother, do you?"

"I've never seen anything to make me think that of her," he said, his voice soft, his hand warm on her face.

"I wish things could be different," Sara sighed.

"At least we can be friends, can't we?" Rafe purred.

Sara's smile held the warmth of the sun and it raced through his veins. "I hope we can," she said shyly.

Rafe leaned in, his dark eyes on hers as his lips inched closer. A sweet aroma drifted to him and he sniffed.

"You smell sweet," he whispered.

"Oh, no," Sara laughed, "that's the fudge." She held the pan out before her, widening the space between them. "See."

Rafe looked down at the dark concoction in the small, square tin. "What is it?" he asked, taking a deep breath and sucking in the smell.

"Fudge, silly," Sara said. "It's a type of candy, haven't you ever had it?"

"Nope, can't say I have."

"You have to try it sometime."

"How about now?" he asked, craning his neck to see better.

"I don't have a knife," Sara said.

"I do." His smile could be seen even in the growing darkness. Carefully, he pulled a slim pocket knife from his jeans and offered it to her.

"What will I tell mother?" she asked, looking back at her log home.

"You won't deny me this one sweet taste, will you?" Rafe pouted.

"No, I guess not," she agreed, cutting a large square from the now set fudge.

"Mmm!" Rafe intoned. "This is heavenly."

Sara giggled. "I'd better go in before my mother comes looking for me." She added, "Enjoy the fudge."

Turning, she dashed away into the house.

"Is it ready?" Prissy's voice met her as she entered the kitchen and slipped out of her heavy wrap.

"Yes," she replied, cutting the rest of the pan into squares.

"Why's there a piece missing already?" her sister grumped, looking at her accusingly.

Sara Adams shrugged offering her best smile. "It needed testing," she said, popping a whole piece in her mouth. "Make the coffee," she mumbled around the rush of sugar.

Chapter 6

Christmas crept into the sleepy town of Biders Clump as snow skidded across the quiet streets and one by one, swaths of greenery wound themselves around porch rails and hitching posts.

Bright tufts of red fluttered on doors or in windows as wreaths decked the entrances of every home and shop along the main street, shiny baubles, or flimsy tinsel sparkling in the sun.

"Town sure is lookin' pretty," George Orson said, escorting Polly Esther along the path toward the pretty little church that sat on the rise at the entrance to the town.

"I always liked Christmas," Polly agreed. "Even grumpy people seem to lighten up a bit this time of year," she said, noting the polished buggy of the Dixon's parked outside the church.

"You think ol' Harlan's found Jesus again?" George asked.

"Only time will tell what Harlan has or hasn't found," Polly said, "but for now let's enjoy the service and that special feeling of brotherly love we often get this time of year."

George sighed, tucking her hand tighter into the crook of his elbow. "You always do believe the best of folks," he commented, patting her hand. "Hope springs eternal, I reckon."

Polly Esther smiled, her eyes crinkling with cheer around the corners as George reached out and pulled on the handle of one of the brightly painted red doors that marked the church's front entrance.

It was warm inside the little white building with the tall steeple. Someone had been up early to stoke the wood stove in the corner of the building, and people huddled together on the straight-backed benches, creating a cozy atmosphere.

A general buzzing sound filled the building as neighbors visited, catching up on the events of the week, and children grouped together, discussing the upcoming nativity play and, of course, the imminent arrival of Saint Nicolas.

"Looks like the whole town's here today," George commented, escorting Polly to a pew.

Polly Esther scanned the crowd for the familiar stately figure of Harlan Dixon, spotting him at the front, his back ram-rod straight in his black jacket. Beside him, dressed in a white shirt and deep blue vest, sat his son, whose shoulders seemed to slump as he turned his hat in his hand.

Across the aisle, young Sara Adams' eyes repeatedly wandered in the young man's direction, making Polly smile and pinch George on the arm.

"Ouch!" he barked in a subtle whisper. "What'd you do that for?"

Polly tipped her head in the direction of the red-haired girl, and George grimaced.

"Best hope her Ma don't notice," he hissed. "There'd be real fireworks for sure."

The first strains of piano music drifted into the air and parishioners scurried back to their seats, quieting in preparations for the morning prayer.

Charles Dalton rose to his feet on the small dais, straightened his frock coat over his slight paunch, and bowed his head as a hush fell over the congregation.

"Our Heavenly Father," his rich tenor voice echoed toward the rafters, "we come before you today with thankful hearts and open ears."

Polly hadn't closed her eyes, and she noticed when the preacher opened one to assess his audience.

"We are humbled by your awesome grace and mighty power, and offer thanks at this special time of year for your gift of eternal love, hope, and forgiveness." He paused as "Amens" drifted through the crowd. "We ask that we'll find it in our hearts to offer grace and forgiveness this season..."

This time Polly noted how the pastor's eyes fell on Harlan Dixon, whose head was only partly bowed.

"...we know that if we will not forgive those who have sinned against us, that we cannot be forgiven," the preacher continued. "Grant us the grace to know when we're just bein' pig-headed, and a heart to welcome all. Amen," he finished in a flourish, looking down toward the little hymnal that rested before him as the pianist began to play *Angels We Have Heard on High*.

Rafe stood with the rest of the congregation as they began to sing, then turned to place his Stetson on his seat and catch a glimpse of Sara, where she stood beside her sisters, singing. She smiled slightly; he knew it was just for him and his heart soared.

It had taken every argument he could think of to get his father to agree to come to church. The fact that it was nearly Christmas and that a respected member of the community should be present to see that all was well in the little town seemed to finally sway Harlan, and together they'd driven to town.

Rafe wondered about the preacher's prayer and its words of forgiveness. Had his father simply hardened his heart toward the Adams for some imagined slight, or did the problem go deeper? A plan started forming in his head even as his deep voice mingled with the others in worshipful song.

"Pa," Rafe spoke, handing his father his hat as they exited the church. "I didn't see the Adams' buggy this morning, did you?" he asked softly.

"What business is that of yours?" his father barked gruffly.

"Well, we are their nearest neighbors, and I just thought it'd be neighborly like to offer them a lift home."

Harlan turned on his son like a bulldog after a stray. "Them women got themselves here some way or another, and they can get themselves right back home the same way," he spat.

At the bottom of the stairs, Maud Adams looked up as Harlan Dixon growled at his son. She didn't know what the boy had done, but she knew that Harlan was the most vindictive, hard-hearted man that ever walked the earth and that Rafe would do well to find it out sooner rather than later.

"Nice ta see the preacher's words did some good," she said sarcastically, as together the men stepped into the light snow in the churchyard.

"You never did know when to mind your own business, did you, Maud?" Harlan's gruff voice buffeted those around him.

"Ma'am," Rafe offered politely, embarrassment creeping up his neck. "I was just tellin' Pa we should offer you and your daughters a lift home." His eyes fell on Sara and she sent him a slight smile.

"My daughters and I are perfectly able to see ourselves home, young man," Maud stated coldly. "We most certainly do not need any charity from the likes of Harlan Demetrius Dixon." She turned on her heel, her head high and back straight. "Come along, girls."

One by one the three Adams daughters fell in behind their mother, but Rafe caught Sara's soft glance as they trudged down the path toward home.

"Mama, that was rather rude, don't you think?" Aquila questioned as they turned into the deeper path of the woods.

"It's none of your business," Maud's voice was flat. "Best to let bygones be bygones."

"But Mama?"

"Quil, Harlan Dixon is the meanest, most unforgiving man you'll ever meet. Now leave it be. It's best that boy of his learns it quick like, too, and we'll all be better off for it."

***

Sundays were always one of the nicest days of the week. Not only did they get to worship with others and catch up with friends, but it was also a general day of rest for all.

Immediately after dinner was done, Maud had excused herself, saying she had a headache and was going to lay down for a bit. Her eyes had been both angry and sad as she gazed at her daughters, and no one questioned her.

Prissy and Quil had each gone off to their rooms as well to work on projects of their own, or knowing Quil, read a book, leaving Sara on her own to do as she pleased.

Bundling up against the cold, she stepped out into the crisp, bright air of a sunny winter's day. Above her a blue sky sparkled, turning the snow to shimmering brilliance.

Sara drew in a deep draft of the cold air and sighed. She'd always loved the outdoors. She never minded the changes of the season, or the sun, rain, and snow. She preferred doing the outside chores to any others. She would have happily done all the milking, mucking, and planting if her mother hadn't insisted that the girls take turns each week with all the chores.

Slowly she made her way toward the barn, pulling the door open and stepping into the dark interior. She blinked as her eyes became accustomed to the dimmer space. With practiced steps, she moved toward the stall that held the family's buggy horse.

The soft creak of door hinges told her that she was not alone and she turned, expecting to see one of her sisters step inside. Instead, the bright eyes of Rafe Dixon met hers.

"Rafe, what are you doing here?" she questioned, her hand still resting on the stall door.

"I was out riding and saw you walk in here," he said, pulling his hat from his head. "I'd hoped we could talk."

"Of course," she said, her heart going out to him. It was obvious that something was troubling him.

"My pa laid into me when we got home," Rafe began. "Told me to keep away from your family, that you were all no-good, conniving women." His cheeks heated as he spoke the final words.

Sara's eyes were wide at the accusation. "But why would he say that?"

"I don't know," Rafe offered with a shrug, "whatever happened between him and your family sure does go deep, though." He raised his head, looking directly at her. "He told me I'm not to step foot on your land, and if he catches me here, he'll disown me."

Sara placed a small, gloved hand over her mouth at the shock. "That's terrible." She stood there for several long seconds, then moved closer to him. "I see you're ignoring his warning, though," she half-smiled at him.

Rafe grinned. "I wanted to see you again," he admitted. "I like talking to you. It's nice to have a friend."

"So we're friends?" Sara asked.

"Uh-hm," Rafe intoned, reaching out and taking her hands in his.

"I do rather like you," Sara admitted, enjoying the way her hands felt in his as a warmth like none she'd ever experienced before ran up her arms.

"I like you, too," Rafe agreed. He wanted to kiss her but knew he shouldn't. Slowly he released her hands.

"Seraphina," he said.

"Hm?" Sara queried.

"You're name, it's Seraphina?"

Sara smiled, "Yes, it was my mother's idea. She's always hated her name." Sara giggled softly. "Mama says her name is plain as mud, and only one letter away from it."

Rafe smiled at the girl's humor but held his tongue, waiting for the rest of the story.

"She said she wanted special names for her daughters, names people would remember. Do you want to know a secret?" she asked, leaning forward and looking up into his dark eyes.

"Yes." He leaned closer, listening.

"Mama wanted to name Prissy Cherubim, but Pa put his foot down on that one," she giggled, and Rafe laughed.

"That would be a pretty tough handle to live with, I have to agree," he chuckled, his eyes shining with mirth.

"So Mama named Priscilla and Aquila from the Bible and me from some story she read."

"Do you mind?" Rafe asked. He was still standing close and could smell her hair. It had an earthy quality to it, like sunshine and wheat fields.

"No, at least mine can be shortened easily," she said, wrinkling her nose. "Poor Pris has been teased since she was little."

Rafe shifted and leaned against the stall door, examining the old mare that was busy munching hay from her manger.

"She came up lame this morning," Sara said, sidling up to him and watching his eyes on the old horse.

"What happened?"

"It looks like a simple stone bruise, but it will take a couple of days before she's sound again."

"I'm sorry I couldn't give you a ride home today,"

Rafe said, his eyes falling again.

"It's alright," Sara replied, reaching out and laying her hand on the sleeve of his coat. "I like walking in the snow."

"You do?"

"Yes, I love the outdoors. I'd ride if we hadn't had to sell all of our saddle stock." Sara looked around the barn, noting each empty stall, her eyes sad.

"How do you manage the cattle if you can't ride?" Rafe asked, wondering just how tough things were for the Adams'.

Sara flushed. "Mr. Brody and his family are looking after them this year," she admitted. "Mama says we'll try something new in the spring, but the herd is small right now anyway, after the sales this fall." Again her eyes fell, and he knew she didn't want to discuss it.

Rafe could see that the conversation was troubling her and quickly changed it. "If you like to ride, you could borrow Chester sometime," he offered.

Sara laughed. "Me on your Appy?" she giggled. "If your father saw that I'm sure he really would disown you." She grew serious again. "We'll be alright," she added. "Somehow we always manage."

"I'd better head back," Rafe finally said, turning to go. He didn't want to leave the pretty young woman there on her own, but there was little else he could do.

"Where'd you leave that spotted horse, anyway?" Sara asked.

"In the grove."

"I'll walk with you," she offered, her eyes bright. "After all, I like walking in the snow." She smiled brightly and it zinged straight to his heart.

As quietly as possible, Rafe Dixon opened the back door of the barn and let Sara step out into the snow that rimmed the woods. A light breeze tugged at their clothing playfully, and he offered his arm to his companion.

Sara took Rafe's arm and walked toward the grove of birch and pine trees in the distance. In the tree-tops, winter birds chirped merrily as they ruffled their feathers against the cold.

Behind a clump of white-barked trees, Chester raised his head and nickered low as his master approached.

"Are you sure you don't want a ride?" Rafe asked.

"Not today," Sara said, stroking the pony's nose.

"I'll come again when I get a chance," Rafe offered, swinging into the saddle.

"I'd like that," Sara replied, running her hand

along his sleeve and plucking at the buttons at the end with a smile as he gripped her hand.

Laying the reins along his horse's neck, Rafe Dixon turned toward home, leaving his heart in the little grove of birch and pine.

Chapter 7

Rafe was kept busy over the next few days, moving cattle to the lower pastures where he could provide hay if they needed it. Being so close to the Rocky Mountains had benefits, but the views didn't keep the cattle fed.

He worked with some of the men who had been part of his father's operation for a long time and soon the herd was settled in wide-open pastures where the snow wasn't so thick.

"If the weather holds like this," a grizzled wrangle said, "we'll have a nice profit come spring."

"I hope so," Rafe agreed. "Seems like some folks aren't as lucky as we are in these parts."

Boden, a long time cowboy, turned dark eyes on his boss's son, smoothing his long black handlebar mustache into place. "You just worry about you and yours and let the rest of the world get on with itself," the older man said.

Rafe smiled. "I see you're in the Christmas spirit," he chided jovially.

"I got nothin' against Christmas, but I learnt a long time ago that you can't help no one, 'lest they want ta help themselves." With his final word, he kicked his mount into a trot and disappeared across the snow.

Rafe studied the cattle as they milled about, pawing the snow to get to the grass below. *Was that really what it was all about*? he wondered. *Had the Adams somehow brought their difficulties upon themselves?*

He remembered dancing green eyes and a pretty smile. No, that just didn't seem right. Sometimes folks got into a mess by no fault of their own. He smiled a secret smile, thinking of the four women nestled in the little log home, and turned Chester east toward the trees.

***

Sara let Saddie into the corral and watched the old roan horse trot a few steps toward a pile of hay. She'd recovered from the stone bruise and seemed back to her spritely self. "Glad to see you're feeling better," Sara laughed as the mare shoved her nose into the hay, "and just in time, too."

A pebble bounced across the frozen yard in front of her toes, and Sara turned, trying to see where it had come from. A pair of white tufted ears peeked over a low pine and she smiled. Looking about to see if anyone was watching, she headed for the grove, her sturdy boots crunching in the frosty snow.

"Rafe," she called in a hushed whisper, "where are you?" She moved around the stubby evergreen and Chester pushed his white nose toward her, snuffling. She stroked his neck that was almost as white as the ground below him but for the large, irregular splotches of brown and black that dotted his hide.

"Now where'd that scamp get to?" she asked the horse.

Strong arms grabbed her around the middle and she barely managed to bite off the scream that rose in her throat, making it a soft squeal instead.

Rafe turned Sara in his arms, smiling wide at the start he'd given her. Her eyes flashed and she smacked his arm. "You could have scared me to death, Rafe Dixon," she sniped, but then softened it with a smile.

"What are you doing here?" she asked, letting her shock turn to a happy surprise.

"Old Chester was missing you," Rafe replied, his eyes twinkling with a mischievous light.

Sara squirmed out of his grasp, moving up to the big horse and placing a kiss on Chester's cheek. "Thank you for thinking of me, Chester," she said, a devilish grin tugging at her lips.

"Hey, what about me?" Rafe grumbled.

"Oh, did you come to see me, too?" Sara asked, her green eyes laughing.

"I guess I was feeling a little lonely," Rafe admitted, then stuck his cheek out hoping for a kiss.

Sara giggled and planted a soft kiss on his rugged cheek. He shivered and grabbed for her hand.

"Come with me," he said, tugging her and his horse deeper into the woods. "Are you going to the pageant tomorrow night?" Rafe asked, still holding her hand.

"Yes, we've all been working on the costumes and decorations," Sara said, twining her fingers with his. "We'll go to town first thing in the morning to set things up."

"I'll try to be there," Rafe said. "Pa won't care if I go to church, as long as I'm home after the services."

"Won't he come as well? It's Christmas Eve, after all."

"No, after what happened at church last week, he told me never to ask again." Rafe dipped his head and Sara could feel his sadness.

Tugging on his hand, she stopped him and gazed up into his soft, brown eyes. They were kind eyes and she didn't like the shadows that flitted through them now.

With her free hand, she tipped his hat back on his

head, then lifted on her toes to place a soft kiss on his lips, hoping to comfort him.

Rafe closed his eyes, pulling Sara close. She was warm and tasted like Christmas, allspice, and spunk. He could feel her hand at the back of his neck as he kissed her back.

Hot breath puffed in his ears as something heavy came to rest on his shoulder and Sara pulled away, giggling when Chester stretched between, them nuzzling her hair.

"I think Chester's jealous," she said, blushing pink in the chill air.

Rafe reached for her hand again. "I'll find a way to see you tomorrow night," he said, studying her face. "Where will you be?"

"I don't know. My whole family is helping out, so we'll be all over the place."

"Don't worry. I'll find you." Rafe smiled, then kissing her softly on the cheek, threw himself into the saddle, and raced away into the trees.

***

"Where on earth have you been?" Sara's mother called as she walked through the door. "You look half frozen to death," Maud added, noting the pink cheeks and rosy nose.

"I was just walking in the trees," Sara replied. She

didn't dare tell her mother about Rafe. She was sure that her mother wouldn't understand, especially after Mrs. Adams' behavior with Rafe's father.

"Well come over here by the fire and get warmed up," her mother said, smiling. "We're hanging stockings." She handed one to Sara as the girl approached.

They'd each been hanging a stocking on the mantle as long as Sara could remember. "It looks so pretty," She said, admiring the fresh greenery that had been laid along the top of the fireplace. The only-slightly-faded red ribbons looked festive.

"I love Christmas," Priscilla said. "Everything's so bright and pretty," she enthused. "Remember the year Pa brought home all the newfangled decorations?" she asked, turning to look at the dark green tree that sat on the far side of the fireplace.

Together the family turned to look at the tree. The deep green boughs were still thick and bright. Baubles twinkled in the light of the afternoon sun as it streamed through the windows. Tiny cones hung from the tree's limbs like natural decorations, and flashing tinsel dripped from each bough.

"It sure is a pretty tree," Aquila said, stepping up and putting an arm around her mother. Priscila did the same and together the family gazed at the twinkling tree.

"What a beautiful time of year," Maud said. "I'm so very blessed to have each one of you girls with me," she sighed contentedly.

Supper was a simple meal that night, but it was made cheery by the laughter and conversation around the table.

"Have you finished all of the sewing?" Maud asked as Quil placed a cup of fresh coffee before her. "We'll be busy tomorrow, making sure the children remember their lines and when to come off and on the stage," she added, smiling as she remembered her girls having their turn in the annual nativity production.

"Yes, Mama," Quil replied. "We even have extra needles and thread in case of emergencies."

"I wish we could have done more," Maud mused.

"If wishes were horses, beggars would ride," Pricilla spoke, the words tumbling off her tongue in a rush.

Everyone around the table laughed. It had been one of their father's favorite expressions when one of the girls would grumble.

"Speaking of horses," Maud said again, "is Saddie alright, or do we need someone to collect everything?" She turned her blue gaze on Sara.

"She's fine, Ma," Sara replied. "I turned her out into the corral earlier and she's walking fine."

"Good. Now let's get everything packed up for tomorrow so we can make an early start of it, then it's off to bed."

As they placed each carefully stitched item into bags and boxes for the next day, Sara added a few extra things from her room, then prepared for bed, but sleep didn't come easily as she remembered the kiss she'd shared with Rafe earlier that day.

Rising from her bed in the quiet house, she walked to her window and gazed out at the starry blanket above. The midnight blue sky sparkled, each heavenly body a bright diamond twinkling down to earth.

In the yard, a rabbit hopped across the fresh powdery snow in search of some tiny morsel, while the shadows of night stretched and rolled over the white crust, bathing the whole world in an other-worldly, purple glow.

"Starlight, star bright, first star I see tonight," Sara's voice whispered into the darkness. "I wish I may, I wish I might have this wish I wish tonight," she finished, closing her eyes and seeing Rafe's rugged face. With a smile, she turned and bundled herself back into her bed. She knew she was losing her heart to the young cowboy who lived only a few short miles away.

With a sigh, Sara snuggled down into the heavy quilts that covered her bed, then closed her eyes and drifted off to sleep.

Chapter 8

"Prissy, did you bring the scissors?" Quill called as she loaded another crate into the wagon.

"Yes." Pricilla snapped, lifting a heavy bag to her sister. "I'm not a complete ninny, you know," she scowled.

"No one said you are, Pricilla," Mrs. Adams chided, bustling toward the buckboard. "I wish we had more to offer this year," she added with her own scowl. "Still, everyone has pitched in and it should be a lovely day."

Sara bounded down the stairs of the cabin carrying two large trays of cake, still warm from the oven, as she smiled knowingly. This year, instead of frosting the dark chocolate sheet cakes, she'd whipped up another batch of fudge and poured the still-hot, gooey candy over the top, smoothing it with a knife.

She giggled, hoping the treat would be well-received, and she knew the fudge topping would set on the cold drive to the church.

"What are you laughing about?" Priscilla asked

suspiciously, pulling her coat tight against the morning chill.

"I'm trying something new with my cakes this year," Sara said brightly.

"Seraphina what did you do?" Her mother's eyes pinned her to the spot.

"I poured fudge over them," Sara replied, jutting her chin defiantly. "You'll see; they'll be a favorite today."

"I hope you're right," Aquila said. "Your fudge is divine, after all."

Sara settled the cakes in a long box under the wagon seat, then hopped into the back with Prissy.

"Ready, Ma," She called cheekily, grasping her sister's hand and kicking her feet. Wishes weren't horses, but at least today a few beggars could ride.

"Did you finish all of your gifts already?" Prissy leaned over conspiratorially.

"Oh, yes," Sara affirmed, "I finished them days ago." Her hand strayed to her pocket where she felt a tight, reassuring lump wrapped in brown paper.

***

The whole town seemed to have turned up to prepare for the Christmas Eve festivities. The blacksmith and the baker were both busy setting up tables with a group of other men, while women ferried buckets, baskets, and boxes of items into the church.

Ladies in brightly colored dresses bustled about the little building, tying sprigs of holly or bits of pine to the end of each pew with a wad of red ribbon.

A Christmas tree was placed in a corner of the raised dais and younger women bustled around it, hanging decorations and colorful ornaments. Outside, children played in the snow, building whole families of snowmen and even a snow horse or two.

Props and a backdrop were set up against the back wall behind where the pulpit usually stood, and a light dusting of straw covered the stage, accompanied by two sturdy bales of hay.

"Everything looks so lovely," Mrs. Roberts commented, studying the stout tree. "You girls are doin' a fine job," the cheerful matron stated.

"Lunch!" George Olson called from the back of the church. "Polly said yer ta come to have lunch," he said a little more softly. "She's made up a big pot a' soup and bread, so ya can all eat," he finished, then turned and stomped back out of the church.

The women grinned at each other, wondering what Polly would have on today. It had become a tradition for her to serve a noon meal while everyone put the church together.

"Do ya suppose she'll make that vegetable soup again?" one woman asked her companions as she shrugged into her coat and headed out the door.

Sara smiled, feeling the excitement of the Christmas Season. The whole town buzzed with cheer. Well most of it, she thought as she followed her family down the hill toward the boarding house. She wondered if Rafe would get away and how sad it would be to come to the play without the only member of your family with you.

She lifted a silent prayer for Mr. Dixon and hoped that someday his heart might soften enough to understand and enjoy the true promise this time of year brought.

The afternoon meal was noisy and delicious as men, women, and children settled in the large kitchen and dining area of the boarding house. Polly Esther had done it again, whipping up a new soup that no one had had before. This year's fare had corn and potatoes in a rich white sauce, with large chunks of crispy bacon swimming in between.

"What story will you tell this year, Ms. Polly?" someone called down the long table.

"Oh, I've got a new story to tell," the old woman said, smiling mysteriously. "You'll just have to listen close and see what it is." The assembled people laughed good-naturedly, wondering if the tale would be an old favorite or a new, made-up story.

Outside, some of the older boys yelled and laughed in the middle of a snowball fight.

***

As evening fell, families began to hustle toward the little church on the hill, their soft, excited voices drifting through the falling dusk. Earlier, women had bustled their jolly families home to change into their best and get their children washed and ready for the big event.

One by one, the families and residents of Biders Clump found their way to a seat or sent their children into one of the rooms that flanked the pulpit, in preparation for the play.

Sara peeked out at the assembled masses through a crack in the door. She and her sisters had changed into their festive wear earlier, and she self-consciously smoothed the silk of her pale blue taffeta. It was her favorite dress, off-setting her hair and somehow muting its reddish hue.

Quickly she scanned the seats, trying to spot Rafe, but she couldn't see him anywhere and her heart fell a little. She'd hoped he'd make it, but couldn't fault him if his father insisted he stay at home on Christmas Eve.

"Sara, Sara," Prissy called in a harsh whisper. "Get the children ready. It's almost time."

The last strands of *Oh Holy Night* could be heard

drifting from the front of the church as Sara closed the door, pushed up the lace trim of her sleeves, and adjusted the head wrap of the nearest shepherd.

"Are you ready?" she asked. The little boy grinned at her, nodding as he lifted his shepherd's crook determinedly.

***

"Come on, boy," Rafe called, leaning over his horse's neck as he pushed his hat down tight, sending Chester into a full gallop over the open snow. He'd been kept late over dinner with his father, who seemed grumpier than ever, and thought he'd never get away.

"Oh, go on then," his father had finally shouted at him. "Go in ta town and watch them silly children prance around on stage."

Chester flew over the snow, kicking up great clods of white powder, his black-streaked white mane, and tail streaming out behind him, as his rider urged him on. The big Appaloosa lowered his head and pounded the frozen ground, zig-zagging around trees and sliding to a stop by the little church as a donkey ascended the front stairs carrying a girl draped in blue.

Rafe raced up the stairs and pulled the double doors wide to allow a falsely-bearded Joseph to proceed.

"Thanks, Mister," the boy of about ten said, pulling his beard down to reveal a crooked smile.

Pastor Dalton rose to stand next to the little tree in the soft light of a large candle holder and quietly intoned as the donkey made it's stately way forward between the pews:

"And it came to pass in those days, that there went out a decree from Caesar Augustus that all the world should be taxed. (And this taxing was first made when Cyrenius was governor of Syria.)

And all went to be taxed, every one into his own city.

And Joseph also went up from Galilee, out of the city of Nazareth, into Judaea, unto the city of David, which is called Bethlehem; (because he was of the house and lineage of David:)

To be taxed with Mary his espoused wife, being great with child."

Rafe ducked into the back of the crowded church, closing the doors behind him, and watched as the boy led the donkey forward, stopping every few feet to ask one of the men a question, but each time the townfolks shook their heads and sent him on down the aisle.

Rafe smiled at the symbolism indicating that there was no room in the inn that night. The boy moved along until he reached the church dais, the little donkey calmly walking along, bearing his burden as if in some royal procession.

At the front of the church, they came to a halt and the boy tried to help the girl down, but she smacked his hand away and jumped down, making the pillow stuffed in her dress pop loose and the assembled chuckle.

Byron, the old hostler, took the lead of the placid donkey and led him away, out the side door as the boy and girl, whose pillow was once more secure, stepped up to the waiting hay bales.

"And so it was, that, while they were there," Pastor Dalton continued, *"the days were accomplished that she should be delivered,"* Pastor spoke, a merry lilt in his voice, as he straightened his coat and looked seriously around at his flock. His eyes sparkled as from a manger placed before them, the very young Mary lifted a rag doll.

"And she brought forth her firstborn son, and wrapped him in swaddling clothes, and laid him in a manger; because there was no room for them in the inn."

"And there were in the same country shepherds abiding in the field, keeping watch over their flock by night."

Sara heard the pastor's words and hustled some of the older boys, dressed as shepherds, out the door and up onto the stage. Several of the younger children dressed in fluffy white followed along on all fours, bleating softly.

"Where's Billy?" one of the Stanley boys asked, looking about him as the sheep climbed onto the stage, arranging themselves around Mary, Joseph, and the baby Jesus.

"Billy," Sara called, in a hushed whisper, "go with the others." She gestured with her arm, drawing the little boy of about three to the front.

Billy grinning widely and dashed through the door, leaping onto the stage. "I'm a sheep!" he shouted, arms pawing the air as he continued to bounce and hop at the foot of the stable, causing the whole congregation to roar with peals of laughter.

Pastor Dalton pulled a large red handkerchief from his breast pocket and dabbed at his eyes, but doubled over once more as Billy's brother, the lead shepherd, snagged the little boy around the middle with his crook and pulled him into line, grasping his hand firmly and shaking his head.

"I'm a sheep," Billy whispered excitedly, tipping his head back and smiling at his older brother.

Pastor waved his hands for quiet, still dabbing at his eyes, and the congregation settled down.

Rafe leaned against the doorpost, watching for another glimpse of Sara as she ushered in the next band of children out onto the stage while he listened to his preacher's soft voice.

And, lo, the angel of the Lord came upon them, and the glory of the Lord shone round about them: and they were sore afraid.

And the angel said unto them, Fear not: for, behold, I bring you good tidings of great joy, which shall be to all people.

For unto you is born this day in the city of David a Saviour, which is Christ the Lord.

And this shall be a sign unto you; Ye shall find the babe wrapped in swaddling clothes, lying in a manger. And suddenly there was with the angel a multitude of the heavenly host praising God, and saying,

Glory to God in the highest, and on earth peace, goodwill toward men.

The pastor's voice was now soft and reverent as girls dressed in white ascended both sides of the stage, humming softly as the strains of *Away in A Manger* drifted into the quiet church.

As one, the congregation stood and began to sing while a sense of peace permeated the little building on the hill.

The singing was soon preceded by three wise men walking down the aisle, bearing gifts for the baby Jesus.

"Still wish we had a real camel," one young man could be heard to whisper loudly to another as they moved along. "It'd be all authentic then," he grumbled, drawing smiles from family and friends gathered.

In only moments, the whole production was over and the townsfolks stood to their feet, applauding the children's work. In a thunder of racing feet, the actors departed to the Sunday School rooms to change and prepare for the next part of the service.

Sara could hear the singing outside her little room as she straightened the costumes and helped the children disrobe. She could hardly wait to hear what Polly Esther had in store for them tonight. The old storyteller never left anyone disappointed, and her tales often contained a thread of truth or a moral that followed you for a long time.

The music was coming to an end and as the children made their way to their parents. Sara slipped out the door and headed for the front pew. At the back of the church, she spotted Rafe and her smile outshone the brightest light in the hall.

An old, dark, wood rocking chair was carried out onto the stage and the lights in the main area dimmed as Polly Esther Olson stepped up, holding her deep purple skirt in her hand, and settled into the chair.

Chapter 9

On silent feet, the little ones of Biders Clump walked out onto the stage and settled around Ms. Polly. A little girl of about two placed one knee on the rocker seat and hoisted herself up onto the old woman's lap, snuggling in close as she placed a thumb in her mouth.

Polly pulled the little mite to her side and closed her stark blue eyes.

"Two households, both alike in dignity, In fair Verona, where we lay our scene, From ancient grudge break to new mutiny, Where civil blood makes civil hands unclean." Polly Esther's voice was soft and rhythmic as she spoke, pushing her chair into motion with the tip of her toe.

A little boy tugged on Polly Esther's skirt, making her open her eyes and look down at him where he sat cross-legged on the floor. "Ms. Polly, I don't know what yer sayin'," he said, his wide, innocent eyes fixed on her face.

The white-haired woman reached out a hand and stroked his head. "Let me start again, then," she said with a smile.

"Once upon a time..." She looked at the little boy who smiled, "there were two families, both looked up to pretty much all over town. They was good people who loved their children and wanted the best for them." She paused, looking around the room to see that all were listening.

"They only had one problem," she said, her dark blue eyes bright with wisdom, "they couldn't stand each other."

At her feet, the children looked at each other, nodding.

"One fella had a daughter who was kind, and smart, and pretty. All he wanted was for her to grow up and be happy. He even had a plan for her to marry someone important that would treat her well and give her all the nice things she could ever want."

Around the congregation, men hummed their approval at such a responsible father.

"It was getting' on to Christmas and folks around the town were having parties and making pies and cakes to celebrate." Polly's voice was like a sigh of silk in the quiet church. "This here pa, he decided to have a party and invited all the people from the town, doin' it up right. The only people who weren't invited was the family he'd been fuedin' with for many a year."

She smiled as if this was the most normal thing in the world. "But the son of the other fella what didn't like this girl's pa, he snuck into the party anyway." Here she winked at the bright, mischievous smiles on the boys' faces. "He wanted to see what all the fuss was about, so he and a couple of friends went to the party."

The storyteller leaned back in her chair, setting it in motion again as the little girl yawned widely, resting her head against Polly's ample bosom.

"There was all kinds of food at the party and this young fella moved around, picking out the nicest things to eat. Pickles, and hog's trotters, and souse."

"Ewww!" Several of the children grumbled, their faces twisted in disgust.

"Oh, well then, cakes, and cookies, and pies," Polly amended with a grin. "He liked them pretty good, too. He'd just fetch himself a cup of punch when out onto the open floor of the big house walked the prettiest girl he had ever seen. She was so pretty he completely forgot about all that nice food, 'cause he had to meet her."

The boys surrounding her shook their heads in wonder, but the women of the congregation sighed.

"Now this boy went right up to her and intro-duced himself, and to put it plainly, she pretty much was smitten with him right away. That night they spent time together visitin' and plumb fell in love." Polly looked around the room, judging her audience.

"About midnight, when the stars were bright and the moon shone like a polished penny in the sky, the girl's Pa spotted the couple and had a fit, throwin' the boy out and telling his daughter that she was forbidden to see him again."

"That ain't very nice," a little girl in brown braids spoke up. "Pa's aren't 'sposed to be rude."

"No, they aren't darlin', but sometimes they can't see past their hurts," Polly agreed, "and this one was sure spiteful to that boy's family. His daughter was all broke up over the whole thing too, but her pa was convinced he was lookin' out for his little girl."

"But if ya love someone, you gotta marry them," another boy of about six-spoke up, grinning at the little girl with braids. "That's what grown-ups do."

The older members of Biders Clump smiled at the boy's sweet words, as many hands were joined in remembrance of early romances.

"Now that little girl was a smart one, so she got a friend to carry a note to her beau, deciding they'd run away together. The young man thought about it and agreed to meet her under a tall pine tree at the edge of the forest. He sure did like her a heap, ya see."

The little girl on Polly's lap had fallen asleep with the soft easy motion of the rocking chair, but the other children leaned in to listen to the rest of the tale.

"They met up under that tree and that young fella took the girl's hands in his, smiling down at her with sad eyes. 'Should we really run away together?' he asked, wanting nothing more than to spend forever with her. 'I know that my Pa will never let me see you again if we don't.' The girl replied, 'I just want to be with you always.' Her eyes were sad, thinking of leaving her family, but willing to go." Polly Esther's voice was hushed.

"That boy kissed the girl's hands all sweet like, but then did something he didn't think he had the strength ta do. 'Sweet-heart,' he whispered, 'we could run away together and I'm sure we'd be happy because we love each other, but if we go, there ain't no comin' back and your pa and my family will sure be sad.' His eyes held sorrow as he said it, but he knew in his heart he was sayin' the right thing. 'I think that instead of runnin' away from our trouble, we should bide our time here and see if we can help our folks heal up whatever wounds they share.' The girl looked at him, her eyes full of tears, but her heart all filled up with love for him."

The little girl with the brown braids leaned

over and kissed the young boy who'd spoken earlier on the cheek, making him squirm. "Eww," he said, wiping his cheek, but flushing at the same time.

"And that's just what that girl did, too," Polly said brightly. "She leaned in and kissed her fella and said that she was able to wait if he was and that someday she knew they would all be one big happy family."

Polly's eyes fell on Sara sitting in the front row, her shoulders slumped as the story struck deep.

"And did they?" one of the children asked, "did they all get along after that?"

"Well it took a while, but them youngin's knew that their love would last a lifetime, so they put their wishes aside and focused on fixin' things up in their town. Ya see love will always find a way and these two, they did. Until one day their pa's shook hands and had a big wedding that made the whole town happy."

Polly shifted the sleeping child on her lap and leaned forward. "That's why it's important that we follow our hearts, but listen to our Ma's and Pa's even when they're on'y bein' stubborn. If we share our love with others, it will always come back to us ten times better and stronger than when we gave it away." She touched a little boy on the nose and smiled. "Now I think we have cake, cookies and punch over at the boarding house," she said, "so let's go celebrate."

A young mother walked to the stage, taking the sleeping babe from Polly's arms as the other children scrambled for the exit, chattering cheerfully.

At the back of the church Rafe Dixon studied Sara where she sat on the front pew. He could see the soft curve of her cheek and wondered what she was thinking. As if she could feel his eyes on her, she turned and smiled sweetly, then slipped away into the room at the back of the church.

***

The atmosphere at the boarding house was bright and festive as people chatted and laughed over the shenanigans of the children during the play or sighed over the tale of star-crossed lovers that Polly had shared.

Pastor Dalton was asked to say a short blessing and then everyone grabbed a plate and moved along the tables that had been set up earlier, groaning under the astounding array of delights. There was hot chocolate for the children and coffee or cider for the adults.

Cakes, cookies, pies and all kinds of treats had been laid out to share, and neighbors nibbled special confections they only had once a year as they caught up on the gossip around town.

Rafe fixed a plate, then leaned against the far

wall of the parlor near a little tree decked in hand-made decorations as some of the older men began to warm up their instruments. With a smile, he nibbled a piece of rich chocolate cake covered in thick, creamy fudge. He would have bet his spotted pony that Sara had made the treat.

Across the room, he saw the object of his affection helping children with their plates, a bright smile in her pretty green eyes. He wished he could simply walk over and take her in his arms, but his mind drifted over the story Ms. Polly had told, and his heart ached for his stubborn father.

His father hadn't always been so bitter, but he'd never been what one could call a cheerful man. He wondered if two people truly could work together to help others find their own joy.

"Did ya hear that?" George shouted, bringing a hush to the noisy crowd. "I'm sure I heard something," he added, cupping an ear and looking about.

Rafe grinned as through the front door a man in a dusty red suit entered, carrying a heavy sack on his back.

"Ho, ho, ho," he bellowed, a pipe clenched in his teeth, "someone told me there were some good little girls and boys here," he winked at Rafe with a twinkling brown eye, "so I hurried over to see for myself." The faux Santa chuckled.

With the wonder only a child can project, the

little ones of Biders Clump circled the man, their eyes wide.

One by one each child was handed a small bundle which they opened enthusiastically, oohing and aahing over little hand-carved figures and a precious collection of candy.

A soft hand came to rest on Rafe's arm, and he turned to gaze into the smiling face of Seraphina Adams.

"Shh," she whispered, covering her lips with a finger, taking his hand and dragging him through the back door.

"Sara. What if your Ma sees us?" Rafe said, real concern in his voice.

"We'll only be a minute," she said. "I have something for you." She smiled brightly, reaching into her pocket and pulling out a tightly-wrapped bundled not much bigger than her hands.

"You didn't need to get me anything," he said, his heart growing in his chest.

"Just open it," Sara chided, her eyes bright.

Rafe ripped into the simple brown paper with a grin. Beneath the layers of string and parchment, he exposed a pair of warm winter gloves, their brown leather a perfect contrast to his heavy tan coat.

As he lifted the gloves, a long strand of braided leather dropped loose, dangling from a thick wooden button sewn on to the outer edge.

"What's this?" He questioned, lifting the gloves in the dim light to examine them.

"Put them on," Sara chivied, excitement clear in her voice.

Rafe slipped the heavily padded gloves onto his hands; they were soft and subtle, molding to his hands snuggly. He turned his hands, watching as the straps snapped back and forth with the movement.

"Be still," Sara barked, taking up one end of the braid in her hand and neatly buttoning it over the deer horn buttons at his cuff. "There," she said, stepping back and looking at him expectantly.

Rafe tossed his head back and laughed. "That is clever," he stated, leaning over to kiss her softly on the cheek.

"Now take them offh" Sara said, practically bouncing on her toes.

Tugging on each finger, he loosened the new gloves and removed them from his hands until they fell from his fingers, dangling from their sturdy straps.

"No more lost gloves," Sara stated cheerfully.

"Thank you," Rafe growled, his voice husky

with the need to kiss her. Running his hand along her cheek, he pulled her to him and kissed her softly on the lips, letting her sink into his arms and holding her close.

"We'd better get back before someone misses us," he grumbled reluctantly a few minutes later.

Sara pulled back, her cheeks flushed from the kiss and from the cold. "You go first," she whispered, dropping her eyes, "and Merry Christmas."

Rafe stepped through the door to the noise of a Biders Clump Christmas.

Chapter 10

"You're terribly quiet tonight," Mrs. Adams spoke to her youngest daughter as they walked into their snug little cabin. Snow had begun to fall earlier and the rooftop was capped with white.

"It's been a busy day," Sara replied.

"I think it was the best Christmas pageant yet," Prissy commented cheerfully, her cheeks rosy from the cold.

"Leave it to Billy Stanley to tell everyone he was as sheep," Quil added with a chuckle.

"He is sweet, though," their mother remarked. "Let's get everything inside and cleaned up so we can go to bed," she added, opening the door.

The familiar cabin was cold as the fires had gone out, but the little tree sparkled in the soft moonlight that streamed through the windows.

Prissy moved to the fireplace, stacking logs in the open grate while Sara and Maud entered the kitchen and started a fire in the stove.

Soon a roaring fire was going, and together the girls washed the dishes, each still bubbling with the holiday spirit that had permeated the service and Christmas festivities.

"Why don't you girls bring your gifts out and place them under the tree for tomorrow morning," Maud suggested, covering a yawn with her hand. "We'll be up bright and early either way," she smiled sleepily.

Scurrying to their rooms, the girls soon returned with packages wrapped simply in plain paper and string, arranging them carefully under the pretty tree.

"Don't they look lovely?" Mrs. Adams said, crossing her hands over her stomach. "We'll have a splendid Christmas," but her smile was a little too stiff and her eyes didn't reflect the merriment of the times.

"I think I'll turn in," Aquila said, placing a kiss on her mother's cheek. "It's been a long day and I'm ready to snuggle in for the night."

"Goodnight," her mother echoed.

One by one the girls said their good nights before trundling to their rooms and warm beds.

***

A soft jingling sound drifted past Sara's window, a sound like muffled sleigh bells in the snow. Silently she rose, lifting her warmest wrap and pulling it snug against the cold of the night.

The solid floors of the little home muted the slight shuffle of her stocking feet, and she turned into the large living room where the banked fire still glowed.

Above the mantle a small golden ball sat, reflecting the golden embers. Sara rubbed her eyes and blinked as she stared at the stockings now full to overflowing. She wondered sleepily where her mother had found the extra stores for so many special treats.

A slight scuffing noise drew her attention as she noticed something moving by the tree, and she ducked behind the fireplace to see who it was. Perhaps one of her sisters had held back a gift or two as a surprise.

The meager array of packages had been so small and simple, they seemed to disappear under the heavy boughs of the evergreen.

As Sara watched, Rafe Dixion unfolded himself from behind the tree, a large sack in one hand as the other fished inside its capacious folds and pulled out a pink box wrapped in a bright ribbon. Another package followed, and she could just make out the patterns on the serviceable but pretty calicos that were tied up with string.

"Rafe?" she questioned, stepping into the room and making him start, but as his eyes took in who it was, his bright smile lit the room.

"Shhh," he said, reaching toward her. "I'm not Rafe, I'm Santa's helper," he hissed roguishly, pointing at the bits of tinsel stuck to his cowboy hat.

"What are you doing?"

"I'm playing Santa."

"But why?"

"I'd think that was obvious." He blinked at her, then he pulled still more items from his bag. "Wait right here," he grinned as he ducked silently out the door and returned with a soft swish of cold air and a heavy box.

On tip-toes he moved toward the kitchen at the back of the house, placed the wooden box on the table, and began to unpack several items of food.

Sara's eyes grew round as she saw first a turkey, then a casserole, and finally two beautifully made pies. She sniffed as warm tears trickled down her face.

"You shouldn't have," she whispered.

Shoving the crate under the table, Rafe

reached out and wiped the tears away with his thumb, kissing her softly on the forehead.

"Darlin'," he drawled, "I'd do anything for you."

Sara wrapped her arms around him, feeling his warmth and kindness all the way through her.

"I don't know what to say," Sara stuttered.

"You don't have to say anything," Rafe answered, holding her close. "Don't you know I love you sweet, Seraphina?"

"I love you, too," she sniffed into his shoulder.

Rafe pushed her away, holding her at arm's length. "Say it again."

"I love you." She offered him a watery smile.

Rafe's smile was as bright as the noon-day sun, and he dipped his head to kiss her, tasting the salt of her tears on her lips.

"You know we have to wait, don't you?" he whispered into her hair a few minutes later.

"I know, but I wish we didn't," Sara agreed, her eyes downcast.

Placing a finger under her chin, Rafe lifted her green eyes to look at him. "I'd run off with you, but I know it would break your heart to leave your Ma, and as cantankerous as he is, I'm all my father has left."

Sara smiled, her eyes bright with love and pride. "Is it any wonder I've fallen so completely in love with you?" she asked, stroking the braided leather strap that suspended his winter gloves.

"We have plenty of time, Sara," Rafe said, pulling her close again and resting his chin on the top of her head. "We'll bide our time." He grinned wickedly, pulling back to gaze into her eyes, "after all isn't that what we do in Biders Clump?"

Sara giggled, then rose up to kiss him softly. "It's nearly morning," she said, "you'd better go." Taking his hand, she walked him to the front door, where Chester stood waiting patiently.

The big, freckly horse nodded his head, making his bridle jingle like bells.

"I have something special for you," he finally whispered, pulling a tiny package from his breast pocket.

Carefully Sara unwrapped the little box and removed a long gold chain with a simple golden band embossed with a heart suspended from it.

She gasped, eyes wide at the lovely trinket.

"I'd like it to be a promise," Rafe said, his voice full of emotion. "Until we can be wed, you can wear it around your neck."

Sara nodded, her heart so full of joy her mouth wouldn't work.

Rafe wrapped his arms around Sara again, liking the way she felt pressed up close to his heart.

"I'll see you in the grove tomorrow," he said, dipping his head for one more kiss.

In an onyx sky the bright northern star, brighter than the approaching morning, twinkled down a blessing on the two young lovers in the tiny town of Biders Clump.

Epilogue

The sound of excited voices drifted from the parlor as Sara hastily pulled her wrap around her and dashed out to where her family was gathered around the Christmas tree.

"Mama!" Aquila squealed, "where did it all come from?"

Maud Adams stood in the middle of the room, eyes wide with wonder.

"Oh, look at the fabrics!" Pricilla oohed. "There's enough for each of us to have a new dress. Even you, Mama." She pulled a soft blue from the pile, wrapping it around her shoulders like a shawl.

"This must be for you, Sara." Prissy rose, handing a box to her little sister. Across the box the words YOUNGEST had been scrawled.

Sara opened the small box to find two simple wooden combs made of pale wood. He would think of such a thing, she thought, a smile etching her pretty face.

"A writing box!" Quil's loud shout had everyone looking as she held up the little pink box full of pen, paper and ink. "And look at this stamp from Sara." She twinkled, dashing around and showing the little quill stamp to her mother and sister. "It's the best Christmas in ages."

"Did you see the stockings?" Prissy chimed, "There's even an orange for each of us."

"Let's make breakfast," Sara finally called, hiding her smile. "I'm hungry."

Together they scurried into the kitchen, only to be caught up short by their mother, who stood with tears streaming down her face as she looked at the meal spread out on the table.

Sara's eyes twinkled with delight at the beautiful surprise. Somehow she was sure that everything would work out alright if she just gave it a little time.

"Come on, Mama," she said, taking her mother's hand. "It looks like we have a turkey to cook. Santa sure has been busy this year."

The End

Author's Note

Ms. Polly Esther, although a fictitious character, gleans her name from a distant relative of my very own everyday hero. During genealogy research, my mother-in-law found a family member who was indeed called Polly Esther. This spritely older woman had been named before the invention of the most infamous fabric that shared her name, and instead of being embarrassed by this fact, embraced it fully.

Polly Esther Olson's character, one we will see often in the little town of Biders Clump, is an amalgamation of so many of the beautiful, open-hearted story tellers I have had the privilege to get to know and reflects many of the little quirks and traits of those who love to share a little fiction with the world.

An Extra Gift: *Never Fail Fudge*

This recipe has been used in my family for ages and is still a favorite with everyone and has been committed to my memory since I was only nine.

1 stick butter or margarine

2 heaping tsp creamy peanut butter

½ cup evaporated milk

2 Tbs unsweetened cocoa powder

2 tsp corn syrup 1 tsp vanilla extract

2 cups sugar

In a heavy sauce pan, combine butter and milk over medium heat. Slowly add sugar and corn syrup, bringing to a rolling boil. Boil, stirring constantly, for four minutes. Remove from heat, adding vanilla. Stir and pour into mixing bowl of peanut butter and cocoa. Mix well. When it starts to lose its shine, pour into a buttered tin or 8x8 pan. Let cool and serve.

If you enjoyed this book check out more books by Danni Roan at http://www.amazon.com/-/e/B013UPZ3IK

Follow her at https://www.facebook.com/danniroan1/?ref=bookmarks

If you'd like to get updates on my work, go to http://danniroan.wix.com/author-blogdanniroan#!books/cnec and sign up for my newsletter.

You can order my books at http://amzn.to/1S9CwVO as well.

Dear Reader,

Thank you for choosing to read my book. I hope you have enjoyed it as much as I've enjoyed writing it. I you enjoyed the story, please feel free to leave a review wherever you purchased the book. Leaving a review will help me and prospective readers to know what you liked about this book. It is an opportunity for your voice to be heard and for you to tell others why the story is worth a read.

If you enjoy Historical Western Romance take the time to look at

https://www.facebook.com/groups/pioneerhearts/

A group dedicated to this genre that offers a chance to know the authors, win prizes, and learn about new books.

About the Author

Danni Roan, a native of western Pennsylvania, spent her childhood roaming the lush green mountains on horseback. She has always loved westerns, and specifically western romance, and is thrilled to be part of this exciting genre. She has lived and worked overseas with her husband and tries to incorporate the unique quality of the people she has met throughout the years into her books. Although Danni is a relatively new author on the scene, she has been a storyteller her entire life, even causing her mother to remark that as a child, "If she told a story, she had to tell the whole story." Danni is truly excited about this new adventure in writing and hopes that you will enjoy reading her stories as much as she enjoys writing them.

Christmas Kringle

Tales from Biders Clump Book 1

About The Author

Danni Roan

Danni Roan, a native of western Pennsylvania, spent her childhood roaming the lush green mountains on horseback. She has always loved westerns and specifically western romance and is thrilled to be part of this exciting genre. She has lived  and worked overseas with her husband and tries to incorporate the unique quality of the people she has met throughout the years into her books.

Danni currently lives in her thirty-six foot RV with her husband and is traveling the United States to see this beautiful country and experience its history first hand.

Danni and her 'every-day-hero' have one son who is attending college and finding his own way as his crazy parents experience the author life along with life on the road.

As a Christian Danni, believes strongly that God brings new challenges, and blessings into one's life to help them grow and she hopes that her words were both and encouragement and inspiration to you.

Books In This Series

Tales from Biders Clump

Sweet, Clean, Historical Western, Romance stories with a twist. Visit the tiny town of Biders Clump at the foot of the Rockies and meet a cast of interesting and exciting characters.

There is action, adventure, excitement, and of course true love.

Christmas Kringle

Seraphina Adams has always loved the outdoors, so when she is asked to help fetch the family Christmas tree she is thrilled, but a sudden accident and a chance meeting with the boy next door change everything in an instant.

Rafe Dixion barely knows his nearest neighbors; a strong fence and a family feud having separated them for years, but when he hears the anguished cries for help he answers the call with an open heart only to have it stolen by an angel as she falls.

Can two, star-crossed-lovers find love in the season of peace, or with their parent's ancient war banish them forever?

Quil's Careful Cowboy

Cameron Royal is a careful man, avoiding drama and entanglements on the open range, but as the years slip by the idea of something more permanent starts to have an appeal.

Aquila Adams, the oldest daughter of the Rocking A range is book smart, determined, and willing to put herself at risk to save the ranch. When the two meet will a careful cowboy and an amateur accountant add up or will the whole thing go bust?

Find out if a peppermint loving bull, a sneaky little sister, and some nosy neighbors can save the day, in this sweet historical western romance.

Brunos Belligerent Beauty

Bronwyn Sparak, a simple shepherd working the hills near Biders Clump, has been in love with the banker's daughter since the first time he laid eyes on her behind the one-room schoolhouse: her fiery hair and quick temper igniting an undying flame in his heart. No matter how many times he is rebuffed, snubbed, or has the door slammed in his face he continues to pursue the only woman he can ever love.

Janine Williams has lived her life in luxury, her every whim catered to by a loving and indulgent father. She has never wanted for anything or felt the sting of heartache, but when a group of outlaws descends on the town, turning her safe life upside down, she starts to wonder if there is more to living than having the things you want.

Can a daring rescue, a quiet pony, and a meddle-some old storyteller help them find their happily ever after or will events forever end Bruno's dreams of love? Throw in the annual Valentine's Dance, and you may just have a recipe for love.

A Teaching Touch

Still new to Biders Clump Grady Gatlin is working hard to be the best teacher he can for any student who is willing to learn. His gentle, quiet nature makes him popular among the children and parents but a busy schedule and a pile of marking cannot truly fill his heart.

Rebecca Carol is more than surprised to find herself the caretaker of the Biders Clump Boarding House, but is grateful for a chance to get away from the shame of failure and the constant reminder that she was too weak to be a useful vessel for God.

As Rebecca settles into her new life, will the fail-ures of the past follow her or can a handsome young teacher show her that lifes' trials are only stepping-stones to something more?

Will Grady figure out the mystery behind the young woman who has come to look after his home before he completely loses his heart or will tragedy dash all hope of joy?

Sometimes you have to go to the wrong place to dis-cover where you truly belong.

Tywyn's Trouble

When a dark stranger rides into Biders Clump on a cool gray morning, turning the town's mind back to the trouble of a few months ago, even the most vivid imagination can't guess his true purpose.

Tywyn Spade has come to the tiny town looking for something he is uniquely qualified to collect, only to find far more than he expected. Through years of travel, over dark trails. the man with the slate gray eyes has seen hard days, but Biders Clump holds a secret that could end his quest and awaken his heart.

Loss is nothing new to Jillian Fort. Strong independent and collected, little touches her in her isolated mountain home. When danger comes calling she answers in kind, but will the revelations brought to her valley shatter her or will she find strength for a new tomorrow?

Prissy's Predicament

Cheerful, sassy and one of the most adventurous cooks in the tiny town of Biders Clump, Priscilla Adams has charmed friends and family alike. Her usual bubbly personality is a draw to many, but when her heart turns toward the town's baker a brush with sorrow dims her usual spark.

Rupert Rutherford has finally found exactly what he's been looking for; a quiet town, far away from the trouble of the past, where he can bake delightful treats in peace. But when he meets the vivacious Miss Pris, he nearly forgets his desire to remain unnoticed.

Could a woman like Priscilla Adams really care for a man like Rupert? A man with a shameful past. Any honorable man would see that the woman he loved was happy, even if it is with another man.

Lucinda's Luck

Young and inexperienced in the ways of love, Lucinda Farrow finds her life turned upside down after the loss of her father. Destitute, she and her mother must make a new life for themselves and only the kindness of their beloved housekeeper seems to offer any hope as she whisks them into jobs at the small restaurant in the tiny town of Biders Clump.

Struggling to find herself in a whole new world, Lucinda finds her life made more difficult by her mother's inability to adjust to her new environment and accept her meager existence, as they depend on the kindness of others to make a living.

After the loss of his sister, Willem Druthers has inherited a farm, a niece, and a nephew but little in his life has prepared him to deal with the after-effects of the children's grief.

Desperately trying to eek a living from a farm that seems incapable of growing anything but onions, he longs for a better way to provide for his small family.

His once-a-week excursion to the town eatery is the bright point in his life, doubly so when a pretty dark-eyed woman comes to work at the Grit Mill Restaurant.

Will fate conspire to keep two dreamers apart, or will circumstances bring them together despite all odds?

Ferd's Fair Favor

Determined to track down the men who left another to die, Ferd Wallace ranges the long hills in search of answers. Unprepared for what he finds, the young deputy from Biders Clumps must find a tender strength to earn the trust of those in need of his help and still put a mystery to rest.

Constance Jupiter, is struggling to keep her Abuelo alive as influenza wracks her tiny home and has little strength left to combat the invasions of her quiet world. Alone and frightened she is unwilling to trust the word of a stranger who's only goal is to help, resisting until it's almost too late.

Can a stubborn determination and an overpowering will find compromise long enough to protect the one they have both learned to love, or will disaster, danger, and past deeds create an insurmountable abyss that dooms them all?

The Travels Of Titus

Leaving behind the only home he's ever known and trusting his little brothers to providence Titus Smith strikes out on his own to find a way to pull his family back together. Desperate for work he falls in with a cattle outfit that shows him the ropes but when rustlers threaten the drive he could lose everything.

Winter's Worth

Rock Bannon has been a member of Biders Clump for a lot of years. A quiet man by nature he feels much but says little. When he stumbles upon a family camped on the edge of the Adams-Dixon Range, his big heart is stirred by their need.

Agnes Ratner has traveled many miles, leaving behind the repression of the deep south and seeking a better life for her children while her husband stays behind to pay their debt for a new start. Feeling out of place and vulnerable as the only woman of color in the tiny town Agnes is determined to look after her family even as doubts about her husband's arrival are wearing her down. Can she lean on a friend as she awaits her fate, or will the trials of time be too much?

Matrice Ratner can see the effects of worry on her mother but finds her own heart on the verge of love when a handsome stranger visits their camp. From the moment she lays eyes on the young rider called

Francis she's smitten. Can a young man on the fringe of society truly care for her or are their differences and the challenge of culture too much?

Life in Biders Clump has never been so busy and even in the heart of winter's grasp love blooms. Will Mr. Williams finally see the light and give his heart to Mrs. Farrow or will his reckless ways doom them both to a life of loneliness? Find out in this page-turning sweet historical read. Come visit old friends and meet new in another Tale from Biders Clump.

Visit the town of Biders Clump. This little town is full of all sorts of interesting characters, sweet romance, childhood antics, and critters with attitude. Love blooms in the shadow of the Rockies.

Rock's Revelations

Rock Bannon has a heart as big as the Rocky Mountains that surround his quiet home, but he's always known that romance wasn't in the cards for him. Instead, the big man does his best to see that others around him are happy and safe. A man riding for the brand doesn't have time for silly things like love.

Mary Ellen Bigsby is off on an adventure to the home of her favorite writer. She knows it is a frivolous journey, but she wants this one trip before she's too old to travel. Having given her youth to the classroom, she's ready for a change but unprepared for what she finds at the end of the trail.

Francis has been accepted by the people of Biders Clump, but the father of the girl he loves is set against him. The young Indian brave will do anything to win the hand of Matrice and start a happy home of their own but can't seem to overcome her father's resistance. When Matrice suggests running away together, Francis has to make the hardest decision of his life.

Will true love win the day or will two young people be pulled apart by one man's stubbornness? What revelations await the quiet cowboy when a tiny teacher arrives in Biders Clump?

Ellery's Eden

After two long months of waiting Polly and George Olson's oldest son returns to Biders Clump but he's not the man they once knew. Having lost his wife, Ellery returns home where he knows his children will be well cared for while he checks out of life. Heartbroken and overcome by grief he hides away from the rest of the world unable to even care for his own little ones.

Ernestine Haven is looking for a new job as a governess but when she receives a letter offering her a place at a boarding house in Wyoming she knows there is more to the simple words than meets the eye. Does she have the strength to take the job and provide for the four children who must be so lost and alone? Will going to Biders Clump prove the answer to her prayers or will she once more be forced to leave behind little ones she has grown to love. Taking the chance that she will find real joy out west Ernie accepts the job but will it prove too much for her soft heart to handle or will it give her the hope and home she has always wanted?

Hester's Hope

Hester's path has not been an easy one, but with the help of her uncle, she will make do on what little they have. Confident her luck has changed when she garners employment at one of the city's wealthiest homes, and despite the reputation of the occupants, she is grateful.

Cecil Payton never wanted wealth, responsibility, or two children who depended on him. He preferred the wide-open spaces of the wild west, but when his brother died, leaving him everything, he finds himself shackled to a fancy house in the heart of the city. Unprepared for the perils of business or how to guide his niece and nephew, he is at his wits end. He can't even seem to keep dependable servants on hand and as the most important event of the year approaches he is desperate to find help.

Will an unassuming, simple woman be the answer to his problems ,or will she too, run from the exuberant antics of his only living kin?

Books By This Author

Qul's Careful Cowboy

Cameron Royal is a careful man, avoiding drama and entanglements on the open range, but as the years slip by the idea of something more permanent starts to have an appeal.

Aquila Adams, the oldest daughter of the Rocking A range is book smart, determined, and willing to put herself at risk to save the ranch. When the two meet will a careful cowboy and an amateur accountant add up or will the whole thing go bust?

Find out if a peppermint loving bull, a sneaky little sister, and some nosy neighbors can save the day, in this sweet historical western romance.

Made in the USA
Middletown, DE
19 January 2022

59158444R00071